A Tale of Six Colors

A KinderColor Series Book

Intercultural Group

At first, there were only three colors --
Blue, Red, and Yellow.

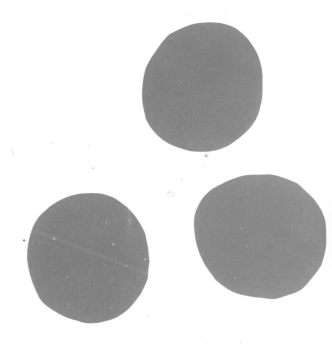

One day, a snake came along and swallowed Blue and Yellow.

As Blue and Yellow passed through the snake,
they mixed together.

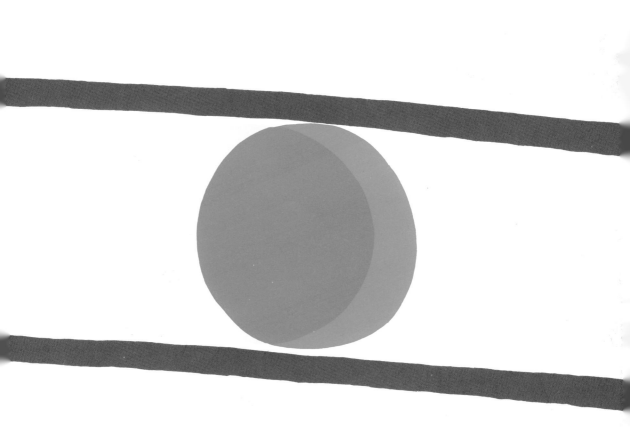

When they reached the end...

Plop!
The color Green was created!

After creating Green from Blue and Yellow,
the snake decided to swallow
Red and Blue next.

When the snake swallowed
Red and Blue, they mixed together

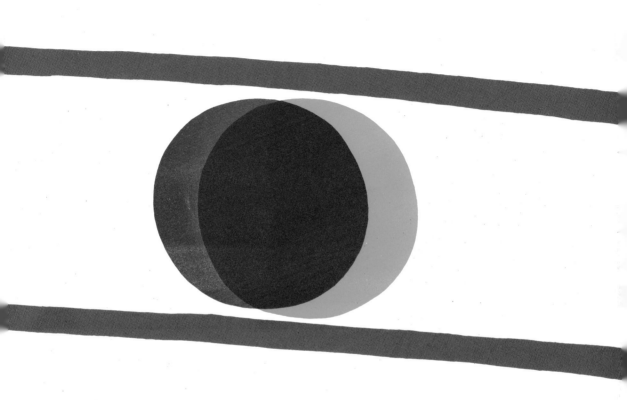

and when they reached the end...

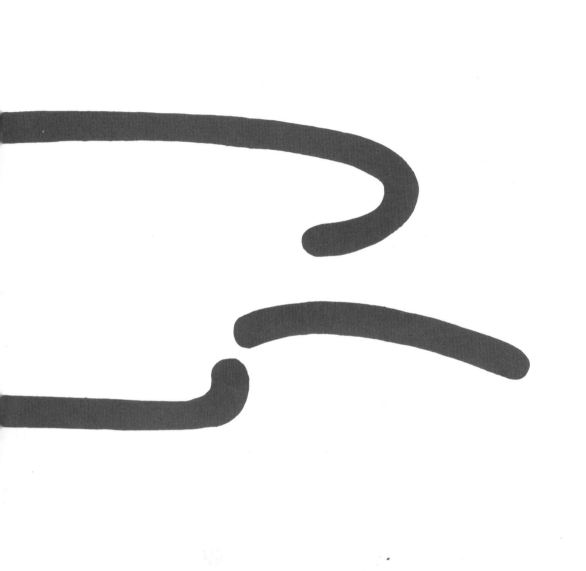

Plop!
The color Purple was created!

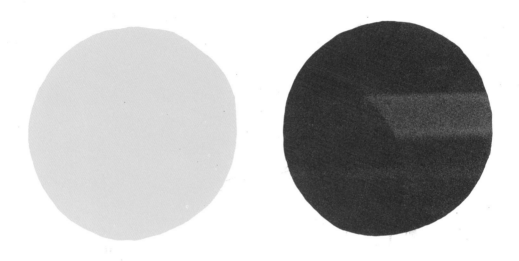

Finally,
the snake swallowed Yellow and Red.

Like all of the other colors, Yellow and Red mixed
together as they passed through the snake.

And, like all of the other colors,
when Yellow and Red reached the end...

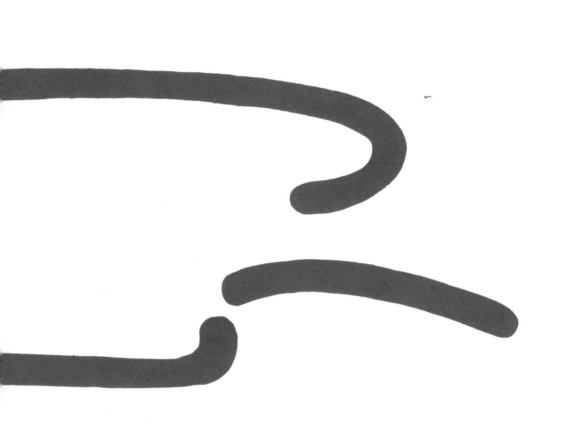

Plop!
A new color--orange--appeared!

From the first three colors--Red, Blue, and Yellow--
three new color friends--Purple, Orange,
and Green--were created.

All six colors--Red, Blue, Yellow, Purple, Orange and Green--were so happy to be together, that they flew up, high into the sky!

Sad because the six colors had flown away,
the snake--very reluctantly--
decided to swallow Gray.

No sooner had the sad snake swallowed Gray than its stomach began to hurt.
"Ohhh, Ow," the snake groaned.

Eating Gray made
the snake very, very ill.

From their happy place in the sky,
all six colors could see the snake.

The colors all felt very sad for the snake,
so each one began to rain tears of sadness.

PIT! PAT! PIT! PAT! PIT! PAT!
Fell the sad, Blue rain
until it created a beautiful lake.

Pton! Pton! Pton!
Fell the Red rain,
causing bright-red apples to grow and ripen.

Poron! Poron! Poron! Poron!
Came the sound of the sad, Purple rain,
which made lots of lovely, little violets grow.

Pala! Pala! Pala! Pala!
Fell the Orange rain and the Yellow rain,
causing oranges and lemons to grow on trees.

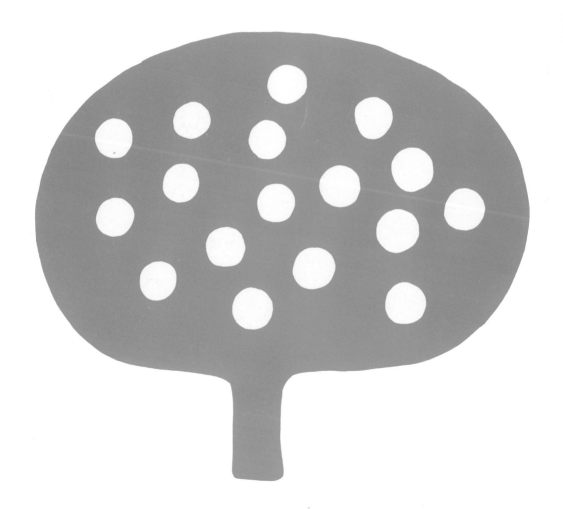

Pilla! Pilla! Pilla! Pilla!
Pilla! Pilla! Pilla! Pilla!
Sounded the big, Green raindrops.
And as they fell to earth,
they made a tall, deep,
and beautiful forest of trees grow.

At the sight of the colors' wonderful gifts, the snake began to feel better and soon became well.

Seeing that they had helped to make
their friend the snake feel well again,
all six colors joined together
in the sky to create a rainbow.

ISBN 1-881267-01-6

Illustrated by Koshiro Toda
© Intercultural Group Inc. 1992
All right reserved.
Published by Intercultural Group Inc.
10 East 23rd Street New York NY 10010
Originally published in Japan by
Toda Design Kenkyushitsu.

Library of Congress Cataloging-in-Publication Data is available.

92-24233

CIP

AC